GRANDPA LAMBERTON and THE GREAT SHIPPE OF GHOSTS

Ships! Ships! Ships!

J (Johannes) Froebel-Parker

AuthorHouse™
1663 Liberty Drive
Bloomington, IN 47403
www.authorhouse.com
Phone: 833-262-8899

Because of the dynamic nature of the Internet, any web addresses or links contained in this book may have changed
since publication and may no longer be valid. The views expressed in this work are solely those of the author and do not
necessarily reflect the views of the publisher, and the publisher hereby disclaims any responsibility for them.

Any people depicted in stock imagery provided by Getty Images are models,
and such images are being used for illustrative purposes only.
Certain stock imagery © Getty Images.

This book is printed on acid-free paper.

ISBN: 979-8-8230-4092-1 (sc)
ISBN: 979-8-8230-4091-4 (e)

Print information available on the last page.

Published by AuthorHouse 01/08/2025

authorHOUSE®

ARTIST CREDITS

All images are courtesy of The Froebel Gallery, Ltd. (https://www.froebelgallery.net/) with special thanks to

Judith Froebel Edmonston

Frances Eugene and Barbara Korr Green

Lauren Young

Alphonsine Thuot Ernst

"Ships, ships, ships!" Grandmother had always repeated when recounting her ancestors who had voyaged to America. Of course, it wasn't AMERICA in those days, but rather a collection of colonies: New England, New Amsterdam, New Sweden and the French who were here too, each vying for an area to establish commerce, protect religious practices, possess land; the reasons were numerous but all sought a new beginning of one kind or another. Grace, as she was called by those who loved her, always said that the land we now called home was more than a home; it was a *City on a Hill.*

That was a "ship story" too. Grace Haskins, as she was called before she married Grandfather, was a descendant of the Winthrop family and a cousin over some generations of Governor John Winthrop who had organized the Winthrop Fleet which had sailed to Massachusetts in 1630. Eleven ships led by the *Arbella* were organized by Winthrop, cousin to her ancestor Ann, who had been in the fleet. *City on a Hill* was a term he used to describe this new world to which he had brought his family, friends and followers. Grace had written out his famous quote for her grandchildren to read in History class:

Now the onely way to avoyde this shipwracke and to provide for our posterity is
to followe the Counsell of Micah, to doe Justly, to love mercy,
towalke humbly with our God, for this end, wee must be knitt together in this worke as one man…

How we had laughed as we struggled to read the English which did not look like the language we encountered in our school books. Grace explained that English had been diverse in *orthography* in the days of Winthrop. *Orthography*, she explained, was another word for spelling.

Her ancestors had known to bring lemons and limes with them.

L. Young

These were available in England because English ships were active in trade with Spain and Portugal where those citrus fruits were plentiful. By squeezing these in the water they drank onboard they would not get scurvy. Although they did not know about Vitamin C, they had learned from sailors and ship captains that the juice of lemons and lime would keep them healthy on a journey which could be arduous even with the best of weather. Countless ships had sailed to New England in the next five years after Ann Winthrop Haskins' 1630 journey. The citrus growers of Spain and Portugal had surely rejoiced at the sudden increase in their sales to English merchants.

A piece of worn paper was one of her treasures kept secure in a latched wooden box with wire rimmed spectacles and a very old, yes, ancient porcelain thimble. It had been folded and unfolded countless times since the 1700s until Grace's grandmother had inherited it from her grandmother. This yellowed and faded piece of paper was not allowed out of the house. She had forgotten exactly who had written down the names of ships on it, but it had come from the family named Clinton, her grandmother's maiden name. They had been on one of the ships of the *Winthrop Fleet* too, although no one could remember which one exactly. Surely it was one of the eleven which she read to us aloud, pausing just a bit as though each were floating on its own breath of air, a wave of energy which emanated from the deepest part of Grace's soul. As we listened, billowy sailed ships glided into our own personal harbors anchoring themselves in the memory of each grandchild:

ARBELLA

TALBOT

JEWEL

WHALE

SUCCESS

CHARLES

WILLIAM and FRANCIS

HOPEWELL

TRIAL

AMBROSE

MAYFLOWER

The latter, she explained, was not the same *Mayflower* on which the Pilgrims had arrived in Plymouth Colony ten years earlier. She could not wait to tell us the irony of that ship's name. However, she had been in deep narration for nearly an hour when we could suddenly smell warm wafts of cinnamon, vanilla, eggs and cream from the enormous pot of rice pudding from the nearby kitchen. "A good story is worth waiting for" was a phrase she repeated often, perhaps as she had so many of them to tell that she could not be expected to relate them all in one sitting.

We were impatient to hear about the "Thanksgiving People," but the promise of bowls of hot steaming rice pudding was an enticement we could not resist. With the expectation of more "Mayflowers" to come, we hurried into the kitchen full of heavy moist and warm vapors drifting from the thick pudding swirling amidst the images our grandmother created for us. The almost sticky mist seemed to imprint those pictures in our memory.

MORE MAYFLOWERS

Still licking our spoons of the last warm grains of sweet rice, Grace promised to continue her history lesson as soon as she washed the dishes. While we helped to dry and place the bowls in the cupboard, she explained that Thanksgiving had always been special in her family. That is why it was as big a celebration as it was in her home with tables placed end to end spanning several rooms. "Ships, ships, ships!" she chuckled as the last spoon was placed in the kitchen drawer.

Although she could claim many passengers on the *Mayflower* as her ancestors, the mere name was a bit confusing. It was a humble little ship which had battled the fierce North Atlantic to reach English territory or, as she pointed out, Wampanoag territory. For historians it was not clear who had built or owned it. Indeed, her Vassall ancestors had owned a *Mayflower* in England where they had served Her Majesty Elizabeth I Tudor fighting against the Spanish. Using their own money from France which they had fled as Huguenots (Protestants persecuted by the French king), the Vassalls had provided two of their own ships, the *Samuel* and *The Little Tobey,* to assist the queen in 1588. For this, Grace said with pride, Elizabeth had granted them an English coat of arms to use instead of their French *blason.* The Vassalls were no strangers to the sea or ships or adventure.

The question remained, however, if the *Mayflower* the Vassalls had owned was the same which the Pilgrims had hired or one which had come ten years later in 1630 with her Haskins and Winthrop families. In any case, her ancestors had owned a *Mayflower* and her guess was that it was the one on which her progenitor, Myles Standish, Governor at Plymouth, had sailed. She had deduced this as it would have been 32 years old in 1620, hence a very "used" vessel which the Pilgrims with their meager savings could have afforded to hire. The later *Mayflower* of the Winthrops would have been newer, she surmised. *The Winthrop Fleet,* as the eleven ships were called, was backed financially by nobles and wealthy English subjects who would have been able to pay for better accommodations and a faster trip on a newer boat. "Ships, ships, ships or *Mayflower, Mayflower, Mayflower,*" she exclaimed with a hint of deserved pride and admiration.

BORN ON THE OCEAN

Judith Vassall, Grandmother's 8th colonial granny, had married Resolved White who had only been five years old when he had arrived in Massachusetts Colony on the Pilgrims' *Mayflower*. At the same tender age as a child in kindergarten, Resolved had already witnessed hunger, sickness, and death on his voyage to America. He had also experienced great joy, for he had received a brand new baby brother born upon the *Mayflower* on December 19, 1620. In honor of this maritime event, his parents had named the little boy *Peregrine*, Peregrine White. He had also been present at the birth of another baby on the ship, this time born to the Hopkins family. Born on the high sea, his parents easily decided to name him *Oceanus*, Oceanus Hopkins.

Grace explained that Oceanus had not grown to adulthood when his death saddened the new colony at the age of seven.

MAYFLOWER COMPACT

Naturally, the Whites and Hopkins had known one another well. Members of their families had signed the *Mayflower Compact* aboard the humble yet noble vessel. The *Compact* was a document composed and agreed upon as a way to govern the Plymouth Colony. The representative democracy in the United States of America today, she carefully pointed out, had drawn much inspiration from this early American document discussed, written, and signed deep in the ship's bowels.

Even Thomas Jefferson, who later penned the *United States Constitution*, could draw personal inspiration from the *Compact*. Indeed, Oceanus Hopkins' sister, Constance, had been the third great grandmother to Mr. Jefferson. How he must have envisioned his ancestor's signing of that early plan of colonial governance as he burned uncountable candles and sharpened bushels of feather quill pens over a century and a half later to compose the *Constitution*, our supreme law to this day.

The connection to the Founding Fathers did not stop there, our grandmother insisted. Constance Hopkins' daughter, Mary Snow, had been the great grandmother of Robert Treat Paine from Massachusetts who had signed the *Declaration of Independence*. Many hundreds of thousands of citizens in America could trace their heritage back to that ship we heard over and over while we were still content after the heaping bowls of rice pudding with cinnamon and plump raisins.

Constance was, and here Grandmother used a Latin phrase meaning an ancestress of a family, *mater familias*, to not only Jefferson but also Franklin Delano Roosevelt, the painter Norman Rockwell, and the first men of flight, Orville with his brother Wilbur Wright.

It seemed that a loveable grandmother's family history and sweet smelling kitchens were a much more pleasant way to learn than history class in school with chalk, blackboards and bells to end limited conversations. With Grace there was always an element of mystery, old faded pieces of paper, cousins, uncles, aunts, kith and kin as well as stories that her grandparents had been told by their grandparents. They had lived in a not so ancient time when people got water from a well, grew their own food, and used horse drawn carriages for transportation.

In an odd way the sensation grew among us that the "dead" are not really gone, but somehow living in another dimension – one not seen and almost tangible when the occasion allowed. In some unique fashion Grace was invoking, almost conjuring up the past so that it was indistinguishable from the present. The untimely demise of seven year old Oceanus Hopkins, born on the *Mayflower* in the middle of the sea, still tugged at our hearts almost four centuries later.

WILLIAM BREWSTER & THE *MAYFLOWER*

Voyaging on the *Mayflower*, which may or may not have been her family's ship (although ONE of the *Mayflowers* was, she always interjected), was one certain William Brewster. Grandmother seemed to know quite a lot about him. He had been revered in Plimoth Plantation and among the most renowned passengers of the ship. She had heard about him from her mother through whom she was related to Mr. Brewster, as were we through her she smiled.

Brewster had been born in a small town in England the name of which sounded funny to our American ears: *Scrooby*. It was located in the county called Nottinghamshire. Brewster had enjoyed a college education at a time when few had the opportunity for such a high degree of education. He had gained immense knowledge from William Davison, the secretary to none other than Her Majesty Elizabeth I Tudor. He had even been the tutor to the queen's cousin, Mary Queen of Scots. Mr. Brewster could read and write extremely well, which was of extreme interest to Grace. Her second home was the Peck Memorial Library in the center of town where her love of reading was cultivated and nourished. She quickly pointed out that it was her fifth cousin, Mersena (Mersens) Brink Peck, a philanthropist from the Dutch side of her family, who had left money for the library and an opera house on the second floor, to be built for the townsfolk.

"Perhaps that is why you read so well, Grace!" We all agreed as we sat at her feet, now rocking back and forth in her mother's venerable rocking chair.

"But what did Brewster have really to do with ships?" we wondered out loud.

Grace insisted, "A good story requires that the listeners understand the background of the story. You will see how Brewster leads to another ship, a ship which may still exist … somewhere."

We had no idea what she could mean. We had no time to question her further, as her narration continued without a beat.

Brewster knew the Bible and could read it in English now that he had been translated into his language from Latin and Greek. The Pilgrims, wracked with illness, hunger and doubt, needed a spiritual leader. Brewster became their moral compass.

Teaching had been part of his professional career, as he had taught English to Dutch university students in Leiden, Netherlands. In Leiden the Pilgrims had created a community in which they could live outside of England practicing their form of Christianity the way they wished.

Grace admired her ancestor's courage. Indeed, he had published religious tracts to send to England which criticized the king and his bishops. King James Stuart was not pleased and ordered his agents in Holland to arrest him.

To escape Brewster went into hiding for one year. The Pilgrims could no longer stay in Holland where the king's agents would arrest their revered pastor dubbed "an elder." Gradually, they made plans to acquire permission to travel to Virginia Colony, not Massachusetts.

Naturally, ships are subject to the whims of Mother Nature "and of course Divine Providence" she quickly added. God, a kind of architect Grace always maintained, had decided to change the Pilgrims' course…"to His Purpose."

William and his wife, Mary, boarded the *Mayflower* with a low profile to avoid any detection by King James and his representatives in Holland. The Brewster children, two boys, were going to North America also. Grace smiled broadly as she informed us that their names were *Love* and *Wrestling*. "Add those to the list of uncommon *Mayflower* names *Oceanus* and *Peregrine*," Grandmother suggested.

"Unique names must run in the family," she proffered," as my own grandfather, your great-great grandfather, was named *Orange*." She would not be deterred from her current storytelling, but assured us she would someday explain, adding in one quick breath that "it has to do with a family in Holland."

Storms had made the Atlantic crossing perilous. Daily the Pilgrims prayed that they would arrive alive in a world they dubbed "the New World." Obviously, ships have been blown off course for millennia, we understood. The same could be said for these Separatists from the Church of England. After what seemed like an eternity, the passengers and crew saw signs that land was close by. They began to detect twigs, branches, and pieces of trees floating in the water. They could not yet see a coastline, but heard and glimpsed seagulls squawking around the ship, as if to welcome them to a strange world which would look nothing like England or Leiden.

Today the peninsula in Massachusetts jutting out into the Atlantic is called *Cape Cod*. Indeed, the waters were teeming with fish of all kinds including cod which Grace still prepared, soaking it in water overnight to extract the salt which was used to preserve it. "William, Mary, Love, and Wrestling surely enjoyed it in Plimoth Colony," Grace suggested. "Especially with wild chives or leeks."

The *Mayflower* could have anchored right there. The passengers were weary of angry waves, water permeating the plaster between the boards of the ship, moldy bread and stale water. Surely there would be something green to eat on land, even though it was almost Christmas. Nonetheless, they persevered further along the coast to Plimoth with its famous Rock.

She swiftly contrasted the Pilgrims' situation with that of those of the *Winthrop Fleet* which had arrived ten years later. In that case, the passengers from all eleven ships had disembarked on Cape Cod and gorged themselves on acres of wild strawberries.

BREWSTER'S KITH AND KIN

Brewster had given spiritual stability to those settlers who thought they were going to Virginia but ultimately founded Plimoth Colony, where Grace's ancestor, Miles Standish, would become governor.

Times were tough. Survival was not a guarantee, and yet Brewster was still viewed as a *pater familias*. Grace told us that that term was the male form of her earlier *mater familias*.

She asked us if we recognized a not short list of Americans. At times we drew blanks; at times we recognized a name from school; at times we knew a person from the movies or television:

President Zachary Taylor (12th president of the United States)

Yes, we knew him from school! His face was on a poster in class.

Bing Crosby (actor/singer) and Katherine Hepburn (actress)

Yes, we knew them from movies we watched on television!

The Rockefellers

Hmm, we had heard that name more than once at the supper table.

General George McClellan (Civil War)

Yes, Yes! That had been on a history test last week!

Henry Wadsworth Longfellow (writer)

Yes, from English class. We enjoyed his poetry!

"You are doing amazingly well," Grace praised us. "But now I will surely stump you!

Jan Garrigue Masaryk? Surely, you will have no idea!"

"Hahahaha," we laughed! "He was the foreign minister of the Republic of Czechoslovakia!"

"How on earth would you EVER know that?" our grandmother inquired.

We answered simultaneously,*"Because our Grandmother Parker danced a waltz with his father, Tomas, the first president of Czechoslovakia in New York City!"*

Indeed, Masaryk had had an American mother and his father had been in New York to raise funds for the new country. Grandmother Parker, "Lina," spoke Czech and Slovak as her family had come from Austria-Hungary. Her father had arranged a fundraising gala which Masaryk attended. As they danced Lina spoke in Slovak and Masaryk in Czech.

"We had no trouble understanding one another," Lina explained. "The two languages are very close."

"Well," Grace pointed out, "your Grandmother Parker was dancing with the father of our cousin! You see, all the people I asked you about are descendants of William Brewster!"

Our mouths were agape as we struggled to imagine Cousin Bing, Cousin Katherine, Cousin Jan, and Cousin Henry sitting together at the ever growing Thanksgiving table. We could not wait to tell Lina that she had danced with the father of our other grandmother's cousin!

Grace's lesson had had a two-fold purpose. It was meant to teach early colonial history and to illustrate the interconnectedness of the descendants of the Pilgrims and Puritans who had all sailed gale-laced seas to start a new life with no guarantees of success or even survival.

The second goal was to draw our attention to Henry Wadsworth Longfellow.

Our English teachers had read his poems aloud for years in a number of classes. We had listened intently with much interest as we enjoyed poems such as *Paul Revere's Ride*:

> *Listen my children and you shall hear*
> *Of the midnight ride of Paul Revere,*
> *On the eighteenth of April, in Seventy-five;*
> *Hardly a man is now alive*
> *Who remembers that famous day and year.*

We did not remember the rest of the poem but easily imagined Paul Revere riding his horse swiftly to tell the colonists "The British are coming! The British are coming!"

Longfellow had ensured that that mental image was indelibly marked on the minds of all of us at school. How we had all longed to be Revere-like: bold, brave, patriotic and useful to a grand cause.

Grace allowed us to enjoy the temporary thought of the American Revolution and then returned to Longfellow, *Cousin Henry*.

How would she connect him to a ship? Was he not born many years after the colonial period and independence?

COUSIN HENRY

Henry Wadsworth Longfellow, a "Brewster cousin," had much of the "Ships, Ships, Ships!" in him. Although his Wadsworth and Longfellow ancestors had arrived later in the 1600s, he also had *Mayflower* forefathers in the passengers John Alden and his wife Priscilla Mullins.

Grace, who claimed Miles Standish, first governor of Plimoth as her predecessor, was sure that Longfellow had been just as fascinated with these early English colonists as she. She pointed out that he had written a poem titled "The Courtship of Miles Standish" which dealt with various aspects of the *Mayflower* voyage, John Alden (Longfellow's ancestor) and Miles Standish (ours).

The ship and the trials of love and journey were all intertwined in Longfellow's work. Poor Miles had lost his first wife, Rose, whom he mourns as Longfellow immortalizes the *Mayflower* story:

> *Tenderness, pity, regret, as after a pause he proceeded:*
> *"Yonder there, on the hill by the sea, lies buried Rose Standish;*
> *Beautiful rose of love, that bloomed for me by the wayside!*
> *She was the first to die of all who came in the Mayflower!*

Miles' anguish was as ancient as humanity itself: a widower falls in love with a young woman who falls in love and marries yet another, John Alden. Grace sounded almost like a parson when she confided, "Sometimes you cannot go back to where you originated, as the place where you are is the land to which Providence has led you for a greater good."

Longfellow had written how his and many of Grace's forebears did not sail back to England when the *Mayflower* left Plymouth in 1621. How they must have loved their native land yet how much more must they have felt bound to the rocky soil, thick forests, and rugged cod-filled coastline of New England:

O strong hearts and true! not one went back in the Mayflower!

No, not one looked back, who had set his hand to this ploughing!

Soon were heard on board the shouts and songs of the sailors

Heaving the windlass round, and hoisting the ponderous anchor.

Then the yards were braced, and all sails set to the west-wind,

Blowing steady and strong; and the Mayflower sailed from the

harbor,

Rounded the point of the Gurnet, and leaving far to the southward

Island and cape of sand, and the Field of the First Encounter,

Took the wind on her quarter, and stood for the open Atlantic,

Borne on the send of the sea, and the swelling hearts of the

Pilgrims.

Longfellow, Grace insisted, felt this strong connection to his colonial forbearers and knew deep inside that he was still connected to them. The specter of their lives colored his world view and shaped it two centuries later. Over one century later, Longfellow continued the tradition in that Americans were reading him to understand early colonial times.

Tonight, after heaping bowls of steaming sweet rice pudding with plump raisins floating, perhaps sailing, on the porridge-like confection, Grace would unlock a centuries-old mystery.

Longfellow had known it too, and Grandmother was awestruck that a distant cousin would have composed a poetic chronicle of her direct ancestor's life. The idea that it would be her kin who assured that another family member would never be forgotten brought her joy, and, she intimated, immense comfort.

GEORGE LAMBERTON, GRANDFATHER
AND SEA CAPTAIN

Lamberton had been born in England just as the majority of the early New England colonists. He was a native Londoner and among the wealthier of the new settlers from across the sea. He was an expert ship captain and a successful merchant adept at selling and buying, trading and bartering with Native Americans, the English in the old country, and the colonists in the Massachusetts Bay Colony where the Pilgrims had arrived on the *Mayflower* and other English settlers on the later *Winthrop Fleet*.

Accompanied by his wife and two daughters, the Lamberton family had arrived in Boston, Massachusetts in 1637. The colony was not old by any means, but it was not new either. Since 1620 more and more English had ventured across the deep to a land which had not yet been tamed. They had not pushed into the forested interior and preferred the coast with its rich supply of fish, whales for oil, and growing commerce of trade.

So it was with George Lamberton who left Boston in 1638 and entered an area close to Connecticut Colony, a new place of habitation called by its name of *Quinnipiac* or *Long-water-land* in the language of the people indigenous to that area. It was accessible to Boston but far enough away to avoid interference by the king if he were ever to send a governor to Massachusetts.

Indeed, the economic fervor that had taken hold in Quinnipiac attracted more and more trailblazers so that in 1640 the population had swelled to five hundred souls. A more English name was sought for the future city, and it was decided that year that it should be called *New Haven*, spelled then as *Newhaven*, as it was a haven in the wilderness and for all who had reached its shores.

Pioneers left its environs and new villages were established, all looking to New Haven as their beacon of example. So interdependent were these towns that they called themselves *New Haven Colony.*

In the center of influence was Lamberton: capable, successful, and enabled to traverse the ocean as a living connection to the Mother Country. He was an icon to New Haven Colony and known well in Massachusetts Colony too. If there was one citizen among the rest who was known by all it was *Captain Lamberton.*

PROBLEMS IN NEW HAVEN COLONY

Although the leaders of New Haven were wealthy merchants and traders it was a bit more remote than Massachusetts and Connecticut Colonies. While the king had given permission to those two to organize as settlements, New Haven had not yet received what is called a charter.

There was little that the crown could do to prohibit the area from being settled, however New Haven could not ask for any kind of support or royal approval. It had no viable military either, which was a disadvantage, because nearby Connecticut Colony boasted one which was sufficiently supplied and trained.

Much of New England, especially in the area where it existed in the 17th century, had soil not suitable for agricultural crops which each settlement needed to feed its population and to sell for money. New Haven was no different and even less fortunate as far as arable land. Those new townspeople who wanted to make a profit and create a new life in New Haven were full of hope, expectation and zeal but realized their obstacles and deficiencies.

Nonetheless, Lamberton and his peers in New Haven were rich in religious conviction. They had suffered in England for their opposition to practices they had rejected in the Church of England. On the other hand, they were not disposed to allowing those of other denominations to participate in the governance of the colony.

Many residents who did not ascribe to the Puritan ideals were shut out of civic life. They could live and work, buy and sell, socialize and cooperate with Puritans, but were not permitted to sit on councils or express their opinions. In their quest for religious freedom, the Puritan settlers of New Haven were stifling insight and talent which would have been of great benefit to the well-being and prosperity of the outpost.

The Puritans of New Haven Colony thought very highly of themselves, according to Grace. They were wealthier than the earlier Pilgrims of 1620, and considered themselves to be the "purest" of the Puritans. They even had no formal government for a time, thinking it was not necessary as they preferred to handle all their matters in the meeting house which they also used for their church.

Grace enjoyed going to church every Sunday, and, of course, so did we, especially when her voice resembled that of an opera singer when singing the traditional hymns, many of which we knew by heart. Things were quite different in New Haven. There everyone was required to attend church, even if they were not a member officially. Non-members sat at the very back of the church or even stood when all the seats were taken. The most important, and wealthy, members sat at the very front where all the rest could see them.

At 8:00 AM on Sunday morning a drummer marched through the streets of the settlement reminding people that they had better be preparing themselves to walk to services. When the drummer began his second march through the streets, all knew they had but mere moments to enter the meeting house or risk being late.

"Grandma Grace," we asked, "did anyone dare NOT to go to church?"

"Oh, heavens, NO! To not go to church was a sin and also a crime for the Puritans. Being absent, except in the case of great illness, was thought to be robbing God of the honor that was due Him."

We temporarily interrupted Grace's fascinating lesson to inquire why she referred to Theophilus Eaton and his wife as Mr. and Mrs. Eaton, but to the miller and his wife as Goodman and Goodie Smith.

Grace smiled and surprised us by giving us a glimpse into New Haven Puritan life. "Those men and women who were church members and had money because others worked for them were given the title of Mister and Missus. But church members who worked for themselves by weaving, milling grain, making horseshoes, etc. were called Goodman and Goodie."

"And if they were not church members?" we asked simultaneously.

"Goodness," exclaimed our beloved granny. "I honestly do not know, but I promise to find out. But if YOU discover the answer, please share it with me!"

Here she paused to tell us a little anecdote about Mrs. Eaton, Theophilus' wife. As she was Mrs. Eaton, we understood that she was a church member and independently wealthy. Grace smiled as she shared a quick anecdote or short memory about Mrs. Eaton, and this soon turned into a hearty laugh. We laughed too, although we had not yet heard the story. Because our grandmother was happy, we were also.

"Mrs. Eaton, whose name was Anne, once heard Rev. Davenport preach in church, and she did not like what he was saying. She went to the Puritan church, but considered herself a Baptist, a church that was somewhat different. She immediately arose and walked down the aisle in the middle of his sermon. She walked past the wealthy members, the goodmen and the goodies, the unmarried men and women members, then the non-members and out the door! Many of the men were shocked, but many of the women secretly admired her bravery."

"Was she afraid of being accused of a crime," we wondered out loud.

"I think not," Grace assured us. "Anne once boasted that if she were rebuked for her action, she would convince 16 wives of church members to leave New Haven and accompany her to Rhode Island Colony nearby. She never did, but everyone knew she would in a heartbeat if anyone challenged her."

The suffering and inability to attain the economic potential which plagued the citizens of New Haven weighed heavily on the luminaries and decision-makers of the commonage. Lamberton was particularly dismayed by the encumbrances endured daily by his compatriots. A man of action and determination, he set his mind to finding a solution which could be exacted as quickly and efficiently as possible.

Time was of the essence, a maxim which he understood well as a businessman. Indeed, fortunes had been made or lost depending on the alacrity with which one could make a viable economic decision. Lamberton wished to enrich both his already affluent family and the entire colony. He must act swiftly.

ACTION

To increase the prosperity of New Haven the founding fathers, with Lamberton's unwavering support, were of one mind to establish direct shipping between their new home and the Mother Country. To date, they had used the "middle-men" of Massachusetts which was neither efficient nor as lucrative as they wished. It was also geographically inconvenient. These backers and investors formed a business society which they dubbed *The Company of Merchants of New Haven.* Finally, New Haven would save labor, time, and money by opening up an efficient trade route with Great Britain.

We were enthralled as well-read Grace made sure we understood every detail before continuing with her impromptu discourse which had now extended over two hours. "There was one major challenge," she continued. "They needed a ship!"

"Ships, ships, ships!" she whispered this time, barely audible.

Her insistence was not at all as vocal or joyful as during her earlier lessons about the *Mayflower* and the *Winthrop Fleet.* Obviously, some element soon to be revealed was preoccupying her. Surely *this* ship would not be blessed either by babies born at sea or cornucopias of wild strawberries eaten by the handfuls on the shores of Cape Cod.

A NEW SHIP

A grand new ship was to be built with space to transport products from the "New World" to willing customers in London and the still beloved Old World. It would not return empty by any means, loaded with all kinds of products needed by the men, desired by the women and hoped for by children, if even just a sweet scarce in the New Haven marketplace.

If New Haven was to have a maritime economy the 150 ton ship needed to be constructed quickly. *Grandpa Lamberton*, as Grace called him, gave his support along with that of wealthy Theophilus Eaton. Theophilus, Grace explained, meant "friend of God" or "love by God," in Greek. They needed the guidance of men well-versed in ship building. John Wakeman, Joshua Atwater, Jasper Crane and Richard Miles assured the shareholders that they were capable of success. Logs were felled and hewn. Carpenters created sturdy beams from the timbers. Canvas was cut and sewn to create the sails which would catch the wind to guide their aspirations across the sea. The trade winds could easily be caught in the tightly sewn sails, but the wood! It was still "green," in other words it had not dried enough to really use for construction. Time was of the essence, however. A "green" ship was better than no ship many believed, but a doubt lingered over the colony like a heavy cloud.

TRADE BETWEEN NEW HAVEN COLONY AND LONDON

The colony needed products from England and the profits, if any, from the sale of their goods in the Mother Country. It was in the now distant land that almost all but the very youngest of the inhabitants of New Haven Colony had been born and raised. What would the English want, and, more importantly, BUY from the struggling settlement? Indeed, it was not yet even part of the larger and more prosperous Connecticut Colony, which it would eventually join.

When "The Great Shippe" was loaded in New Haven harbor its cargo was full of the only, although desirable products which the colony could produce. Many of the planters had been growing a vegetable highly prized in England. They had brought peas with them across the Atlantic to plant in their new home. They grew well and did not need the rich soil which cotton or tobacco required in places such as Virginia Colony. Peas were valuable as food as they could be dried, stored and used throughout the English winter when it was almost impossible to find fresh vegetables. Green peas were a popular food all over the kingdom. Surely the London merchants would pay a good price for them. At this point, Grace interjected that split pea soup was still one of her favorites to make especially on cold, damp days!

Even at a very good selling price, a ship full of peas would not make enough money to pay for the building of the ship, salaries for the crew, and pay for the products from England that the colonists needed and wanted. The investors who had used their money to finance the ship's construction also had to be repaid, so it was important to get to London as quickly as possible, make a profit and return with a cargo of English goods and much needed revenue.

Indeed, the men who had risked their money to build the ship had formed a new company to do so. They called themselves "The Ship Fellowship." They were keen to be repaid, however, and to make a profit. They urged the shipbuilders to work as quickly as possible, knowing full well that the wood was not yet in perfect condition to use. Never mind, they surely thought. With the money we make on this rapid journey, we will build a better ship and give it a proper name. Then we will build an entire fleet to make many voyages every year! Their dreams of success clouded their better judgment we shall soon see.

Another crop which seemed to grow well in the soil and climate of New Haven was buckwheat. Grandma Grace assured us that it was really not wheat at all. Wheat grew on a plant which looked like high grass, but buckwheat, although it had "wheat" in its name, it was not at all a cereal. On the other hand, it was used like cereal and was highly nutritious. The closest thing that Grace could think of was a plant from South America called quinoa, but she had never eaten it, though if she could find it, she promised, she would be happy to prepare it for us to try. Buckwheat would be easier to find, and she had recipes her family had prepared with it for many generations.

Hides from goats, cattle, deer and beaver were also very prized in England. New Haven had plenty of that from the animals on its farms and also the unlimited supply of deer in the nearby forests. The rivers were full of beaver which was used to make coats, hats and line other garments to keep the English warm in the many months of cold, damp weather. So all of these were added to the cargo being loaded every day in the harbor. Perhaps even King Charles I would sit upon a fancy new chair upholstered with New Haven hides, or even sport a coat on his famous fox and quail hunts lined with beaver fur from America. The possibilities were limitless as soon as "The Great Shippe" could arrive and unload its precious cargo.

"MAN SHALL NOT LIVE BY BREAD ALONE"

"Man shall not live by bread alone," Grace often said throughout her life. She repeated the phrase just here, and we knew immediately that she was preparing us for another insight into the story of "The Great Shippe."

One of New Haven's founding fathers was Reverend John Davenport who was a minister, a pastor in the Puritan Church, later called the Congregational Church.

The services in the Puritan Church were much plainer than in the Church of England. The people of New Haven had left England for many reasons, but one was that the king was not happy with them as they did not like to go to his church and criticized those things about it which they did not like. They wanted to be in New Haven where they could worship and understand God the way they chose. Although they respected the king, they also liked their liberty when it came to church. Reverend Davenport was a great scholar, a theologian who studies and writes about the Bible and religion. Puritan sympathizers in

England, as well as those opposed to the Puritan Church, wanted to read all the things that Reverend Davenport had written. His sermons, essays and other publications were loaded on the ship right next to the peas and buckwheat. "Food for the body next to food for the soul," Grace commented.

READY TO LEAVE

The ship was finally ready to leave New Haven, but Mother Nature, as some called the weather, did not cooperate. It was in January of the year 1647 that the departure had been marked on their calendars knowing that arriving before that would not be fruitful as the majority of Englishmen and women would be celebrating Christmas for 12 days. Nobody would be transacting business during that time. Weighing 150 tons the ship was ready but the harbor was suddenly not navegable, as a period of arctic cold had gripped the struggling settlement for the weeks prior. "The Great Shippe" was totally encased in ice!

Even the native inhabitants of that region, the Quinnipiac people, could not remember a colder winter nor could the elders of the tribe. As the entire population of New Haven relied on the business of trade with England, they knew they must work together as a community. Every able bodied man, young and old and even a few stout boys, took their axes, picks and other tools as they had at their disposal to the harbor. In the bitter cold they worked tirelessly during the day. At night they used the light of torches to continue laboring in shifts until a three mile channel to Long Island Sound had been hacked open. Once in the sound, or larger waterway, they still had to get to the Atlantic Ocean to fill the sales with the winds which would push them to England.

When the arduous journey through the jagged channel allowed Captain Lamberton, crew and passengers to make it to the sound, there was still not enough wind to move them. At this point, the ship was towed by other vessels backwards until the ocean! With shouts of gratitude from Grandpa Lamberton and the shouted well wishes of those who would return to New Haven, the ship, *cranky* and *walty* as many called its lopsidedness, entered the unpredictable and abnormally turbulent waters of the Atlantic Ocean.

Suddenly, a shudder shot through Captain Lamberton, Grace's and our ancestor. It entered from the tip of his head like a bolt of icy lightning, resting for an unpleasant moment in his chest as though the churning ocean were inside of him. Just as swiftly as it had penetrated his body, it shot out of his feet as though he had been connected to an experiment by Benjamin Franklin almost one hundred years later. This unanticipated, almost supernatural experience changed Grandpa Lamberton's entire view of "The Great Shippe," what kind of a vessel it was, where it would travel, what its final destination would be, and, truly, what the fate of all aboard would be. Grace said that Captain Lamberton was "prescient," a new vocabulary word meaning that he could see into the future and understand that which would take place before it happened.

"SHE SHALL PROVE OUR GRAVE"

To prove her point, Grace quoted a statement that many in New Haven had heard Captain Lamberton utter before boarding the vessel, " She shall prove our grave!" Lamberton was not alone, as Governor Winthrop from the Massachusetts Colony had also claimed, "The Shippe never went voyage before and was verye cranckesided!' Being lopsided was indeed a troublesome fact, but the added weight of all those peas, hides and buckwheat were surely going to make the situation worse!

NO NEWS IS BAD NEWS

Months went by without any word about "Grandpa Lamberton," known to the seventy members of the passengers and crew simply as "Captain Lamberton." Evey ship from England which arrived from London was anticipated at the docks when they anchored. In hushed voices, the townspeople, in particular Reverend Davenport, would implore the crew if they had seen "The Great Shippe" in London. Indeed, it had never returned to New Haven filled to the brim with English products and interminable stories by all about their adventures, successes and failures in England. Where could they be? The answers never varied in their content, for no one had ever seen Lamberton's vessel once it had sailed out of sight upon exiting Long Island Sound.

With deep regret, greater sadness, sorrow, mourning many bewailed the truth which was becoming clear and inevitable: "The Great Shippe" had never reached land and was surely at the bottom of the ocean. Surely, all the loved ones of New Haven who had left on the ship would never ever be seen again. Many knelt privately in prayer in their homes, and in the congregational meetings of the Puritan Church.

At this point, they no longer had hope that anyone aboard could have survived the disaster. It was surely as definite and unequivocal as had been the defeat of the Spanish Armada under the queenship of Her Majesty Elizabeth I. It could not be denied by anyone. However, the Puritans were a people of deep faith, not to be discouraged.

"THE LORD HEARS THE PRAYERS OF THE RIGHTEOUS"

Sunday after Sunday Reverend Davenport exhorted his congregation not to abandon hope. Grace explained that the believers felt they must give thanks to the Creator even in the face of sadness. Had Moses not given an example to be followed even now when the Hebrews wandered in the desert before reaching the Promised Land? Although difficult, gratitude for everything even when one was sad was still possible. Did the Puritans not sing the Doxology in every Sunday service, "Praise God from Whom all blessings flow, praise him all creatures here below?"

Indeed, Davenport continually reminded his flock of followers that "The Lord hears the prayers of the righteous," and the New Haveners were righteous in their private and public lives. Yet, it was a struggle to be joyous knowing that seventy souls had perished in the cold, turbulent and unpredictable sea. The resilient inhabitants of New Haven persevered.

THE WINTER ENDS

The frigid winter slowly ebbed to the insistence of Spring. There was still snow in the shady, rocky areas of the open fields, but each day less. The frozen streams now gurgled with snow visible only in the shadiest nooks and crannies of the brooks where trout were now seen bringing a new food source to the community after the salted cod which the cooks of New Haven had eaten all winter. Where white and grey had been the predominant colors since the departure of "The Great Shippe," yellow daffodils, white jonquils, and vibrant tulips from the Netherlands, began to insist in their attempt to chase away the blandness of the past winter.

Life began to show itself anew as the days became longer and the weather more pleasant. Windows were suddenly opened, and feather beds and pillows could be placed in them every morning to let them soak in the fresh air, making even sleeping more comfortable. Neighbors who had not seen much of each other during the winter, suddenly emerged from their houses. They shared conversations in the streets, in the market, at the dock fishing, at the brook when doing the laundry, and even after Sunday services as they walked home.

Some had dreams about "The Great Shippe" claiming to have seen a great wave swallowing it up in one fell swoop. Another claimed an angel had appeared either in a dream or half awake, telling the neighbor that the community should not fear. All of these stories and accounts circulated wildly throughout the settlement, all reaching Reverend Davenport who never criticized them, never corrected, and never belittled them.

There was not a citizen in the colony who did not have some connection to those who had left that last icy January from New Haven harbor. The event left absolutely no one unscathed, and, as all were faithful and believed in God, all prayed every day, every Sunday, every moment when one had a quiet personal devotion. In this petition to the Divine they were of one mind and one plea, " Dear Lord, show us the fate of our loved ones who we commit to thy majesty!"

A HUMID SUMMER

The Quinnipiac neighbors had told Reverend Davenport and others that the intense cold of the past winter foretold a hot and humid summer to come. Indeed, the Creator of the Universe had a way of "evening things out" with times of drought followed by rain, icy winters followed by sweltering summers, an autumn filled with copious blackberries followed by another with scarce supply. There was balance in all of life! Grace explained, "The Lord giveth, and the Lord taketh away." The very pleasant spring became warmer and rainier. By June of 1647 thunder and lightning coming off the ocean seemed to be the rule rather than the exception most days of the week.

The wells were filling up for which most were thankful! There had been times in the past when they were drier than they were wet! Now there seemed to be water in everyone's well and rain in abundance for the crops including the peas, which were planted each year in the light of the first full moon after Good Friday, a custom from the Olde Worlde brought by the Puritans. Nobody knew exactly why, but the old-timers insisted that peas planted in the moonlight seemed to grow better! As it was a custom, many in New Haven looked forward to this ritual, regardless of whether the peas grew better or not. No one knew as they had always planted peas this way, even in the Motherland.

Grace had heard from her grandmother who had heard it from hers that the storms in New Haven that summer of 1647 seemed to grow in intensity. The lightning each day a bit more spectacular was accompanied by louder and louder booms of thunder which echoed across the colony. The phenomenon became so prevalent that more than a few wondered if a celestial event was being heralded with the claps of thunder like the trumpets of angels in Bethlehem so long ago.

One day the sky cleared completely. Blue heavens opened up over the village. The muddy streets dried, and children played outside barefoot without having to worry if their mother would scold them for their muddy feet when they came home. There was hardly a whisper of a breeze which all noted as the many days preceding had been gusty, indeed gustier each day. Now silence. Not a breath of air. The seagulls' could be heard screeching louder than ever as there was absolute silence in the harbor except for the water lapping at the rocks and stones on the shore. Grandpa Lamberton's wife, Margaret, Grandma Margaret or *Grandma Maggie* as Grace might call her, was the first to note the swift change. She found it somewhat unsettling as she remembered the old adage, "A clear sky is beautiful, but when there are no clouds above, a storm is sure to follow." Indeed, the next morning at dawn the sky was a beautiful pinkish grey on the horizon causing Grandma Lamberton to quote the mariners who had always been part of life in London and now New Haven Colony: "Red sky at night sailors delight. Red sky in the morning, sailors take warning!"

A STORM OF MAGNITUDE

At about noon the clouds in the harbor changed from light grey to dark, almost steel grey, and then finally to black. The sailors who had traveled to the Bahamas and Caribbean muttered that the sudden shift in weather reminded them of the hurricanes that had threatened their ships and lives at various times in their careers. Suddenly the wind began to gale as never before. It was so fierce that many knelt to pray in their homes in which they had shuttered and latched the windows. Their pleas were that Providence would deliver them from the impending tempest.

The first intense gust felled trees around the perimeter of the settlement. Even in their houses the falling trees and snapping branches could be heard. More than a few roofs received the impact and caused the foundations to rattle and the inhabitants to hide under their beds. So audible and fierce was the sound of the falling trees, the same used for the masts of "The Great Shippe, that more than one New Havener, including Grandma Margaret, could not help thinking of how the masts of the vessel had surely broken and snapped before it sank with their seventy loved ones on board. A Quinnipiac native who had taken refuge under a rock overhang by the shore told a Puritan through an interpreter, another Quinnipiac who could speak that language and English, that it seemed that an army was banging the gates and walls of an invisible fort trying to enter by force. The thunder became more ominous and repetitious. The lightning lit up the sky as though a portal between Heaven and Earth had opened. It was then that the Quinnipiac witness was the first to observe that in the sky a specter was beginning to take shape. He confided this to the interpreter who at first insisted that he could see nothing but angry clouds moving as though in a kind of phantasmagorical dance, one which reminded him of those performed at certain times of year in the Quinnipiac villages.

"THE GREAT SHIPPE" APPEARS

When the interpreter had also seen it, he left his friend and the Puritan with them and ran to Reverend Davenport's abode. He knocked on the door with such insistence that the good minister was momentarily stunned. "What is wrong, dear friend? Why hast Thou sought me?"

The interpreter insisted, "Good Reverend, make haste to the harbor, "The Great Shippe" is coming back, coming back. It doth float in the sky!" Before hastily grabbing his coat and hat, Reverend Davenport, who never had ever doubted that the Creator of All Things had abandoned the ship or the good people of New Haven, said a quick prayer, "Dear Lord, Thy Holy Will be done on Earth as it is in Heaven! Amen!"

Along the way, the rain having somewhat subsided, the good pastor of the community yelled for the neighbors, his flock of believers, to follow to the water. "Make haste! The Lord speaketh in the clouds!" As more and more gathered at the shore, on the docks and on the rocks near the water, a ghostly apparition became clearer and clearer. It was indeed a ship, but not just any ship, rather definitely "The Great Shippe!" Its construction had been so well known to the entire populace that they could not confuse it with any other ship!

The specter of the sea vessel had not disappeared even after five minutes. It was surely not a figment of any imagination as it lingered as though by design so that the townspeople could be sure that they were all seeing the same apparition. Suddenly, Grandma Lamberton, shouted that she saw a man on board with a sword pointing toward Heaven. Indeed, all saw the same thing. As captain, Grandpa Lamberton, her husband, had taken his sword also on the voyage. Could it be him! Maggie adjusted her wire rimmed glasses and was sure it was her husband, but how could this be? Was he not dead? She suddenly remembered Reverend Davenport's having preached many times about the Communion of Saints, that the believers on Earth and the believers in Heaven were all alive in faith. Life was eternal although in different ways at different times. She became calm at this memory.

Not only the people on the shore were witnessing the ship but other ships in the harbor were privy to a similar vision from a unique perspective. While the townspeople could see "The Great Shippe" in the clouds every more clearly, the mariners were having an even more intense experience. They were anchored in the harbor and had come out on deck as the rain subsided to check their masts and sails for damage after the intense thunderstorm. To their amazement "The Great Shippe" pulled up next to their vessels. So close, many later recounted, that it seemed they could reach across to the other deck to shake hands with the passengers and crew on deck, including Captain Lamberton. They clearly recognized those who had left New Haven through the icy channel only to be towed backwards through Long Island Sound. Why, some on deck even smiled at the sailors who were mesmerized yet flabbergasted. They asked one another, "Were not these souls lost at sea? How have they returned from the depths of the ocean in bodies that we can see and almost touch? Were we wrong? Did they survive and return from London?"

"THE GREAT SHIPPE DISAPPEARS"

Fifteen minutes had passed and the ship was still visible. There was no doubt that the prayers of the faithful had been answered in a mysterious yet glorious way. All in New Haven saw the same specter, although from unique perspectives. When later the sailors and townspeople spoke with one another, the emerging story left no doubt, the mortal souls who had left New Haven had entered swiftly into eternity on the ocean but had not forgotten that their loved ones in the settlement were grieving. They had been given a special grace to return in a kind of triumphant announcement that their voyage had not led them to London, but rather to Heaven itself.

Without fanfare and without warning the sails of the ship were taken in and the masts fell one after the other, the passengers and crew became invisible and the ship gradually returned to the clouds and mist which had heralded its arrival.

CONSENSUS

There was immediate consensus amongst the townsfolk. A godly vision had been granted them, one which they would never forget and one which would become a legend in the oral traditions of all the families who witnessed it. Reverend Davenport immediately wrote a letter to Governor Winthrop of the Massachusetts Colony informing him of the miraculous events of the day. He had continually assured his congregation to never abandon hope and to bring their petitions to the Almighty with the expectation that His Will would be theirs and their will His. In his Sunday sermon after the miracle, he proclaimed from the pulpit, "God had descended for the quieting of our afflicted spirits, this extraordinary account of sovereign disposal of those for whom so many fervent prayers were made continually."

THE PORCELAIN THIMBLE

With that our grandmother, Grace, laid down the ancient thimble which she had kept in her hand during the entire lesson. She carefully unfolded the rest of the fragile paper which she had previously opened partially while reading the names of ships from the Winthrop Fleet. She now revealed the rest of its contents. It contained a family tree which showed how she, and now we, were descended from Grandpa and Grandma Lamberton. Indeed, we were descendants of their daughter, perfectly named "Mercy." Mercy Lamberton had married an Englishman named Shubael Painter with whom they had had a daughter, another Margaret named after her widowed Grandmother Lamberton. Margaret then married a Lawrence Clinton who could count as his ancestors the Earls of Lincoln. His father had come to the Massachusetts Colony but returned, leaving young Lawrence to build a life in this untamed "New World," new to the English but not new to the native inhabitants who had been here for centuries before. Generations of Clintons led to the Haskins, Grandmother Grace's maiden name. Indeed, the Haskins had come with Governor Winthrop whose cousin, Anne, had married into the family.

"And when I someday am in the same world where Grandpa Lamberton and "The Great Shippe of Ghosts" reside in Heaven one of you will guard this precious paper and add to it all who shall come afterwards."

"And the thimble?" we all inquired simultaneously.

"Ah," she thoughtfully replied, "This was Grandma Maggie Lamberton's. She was a talented seamstress and used it while fashioning a linen shirt, trousers and top coat for Grandpa Lamberton when he reached London. He wanted to impress the merchants of that city whom he hoped to convince to buy his goods from New Haven. He never reached his destination as we know. But when I put on the thimble I can feel all the love Maggie had for George. Every stitch, every hem, every eyelet. These clothes most surely went to the bottom of the sea with the doomed passengers and crew."

She paused and quickly added, "OR he was wearing them Maggie saw him onboard with the other ghostlike passengers when the ship appeared in New Haven. This is the version I prefer, as he would have proven to her that her labors were not in vain and that her needlework would be worn for all eternity."

HENRY WADSWORTH LONGFELLOW'S
POEM "THE PHANTOM SHIP"

"Before I send you home with rice pudding for your parents to enjoy, I do want to recite to you the short poem which Longfellow penned to immortalize Grandpa Lamberton, that is Captain Lamberton, and those who met their earthly end on the high seas in "The Great Shippe.""

In Mather's Magnalia Christi,

Of the old colonial time,

May be found in prose the legend

That is here set down in rhyme.

A ship sailed from New Haven,

And the keen and frosty airs,

That filled her sails at parting,

Were heavy with good men's prayers.

'O Lord! if it be thy pleasure'--

Thus prayed the old divine--

'To bury our friends in the ocean,

Take them, for they are thine!'

But Master Lamberton muttered,

And under his breath said he,

'This ship is so crank and walty

I fear our grave she will be!'

And the ships that came from England,

When the winter months were gone,

Brought no tidings of this vessel

Nor of Master Lamberton.

This put the people to praying

That the Lord would let them hear

What in his greater wisdom

He had done with friends so dear.

And at last their prayers were answered:--

It was in the month of June,

An hour before the sunset

Of a windy afternoon,

When, steadily steering landward,

A ship was seen below,

And they knew it was Lamberton, Master,

Who sailed so long ago.

On she came, with a cloud of canvas,

Right against the wind that blew,

Until the eye could distinguish

The faces of the crew.

Then fell her straining topmasts,

Hanging tangled in the shrouds,

And her sails were loosened and lifted,

And blown away like clouds.

And the masts, with all their rigging,

Fell slowly, one by one,

And the hulk dilated and vanished,

As a sea-mist in the sun!

And the people who saw this marvel

Each said unto his friend,

That this was the mould of their vessel,

And thus her tragic end.

And the pastor of the village

Gave thanks to God in prayer,

That, to quiet their troubled spirits,

He had sent this Ship of Air.

Not long after this evening of rice pudding and tales of ships, ships, ships, Grace went to the same eternal home as Grandpa and Grandma Lamberton. Captain Lamberton surely gave her a tour of the vessel and explained to her finally in full the true events of that fateful journey to London. She, in turn, would have assured them that her grandchildren, his descendants, knew of him very well and would be sure to tell the story for generations to come of that miraculous reappearance in and above the harbor of New Haven.

AUTHOR BIOGRAPHY

J (Johannes) Froebel-Parker continues to add to the growing list of titles in his Ahnentafel Book Series (ahnentafelbooks.com) which includes *Grand Duchess Anastasia: Still a Mystery*? (Histria Books, 2023) available at histriabooks.com/product/grand-duchess-anastasia.

His stories deal with characters of historical importance from paternal and maternal family trees, which include Tudors, victims of the Salem Witch Hysteria, educators such as Friedrich Froebel (Kindergarten), and theologians (Rev. John Rogers, the Martyr). He attended Marathon Central School in Marathon, New York and studied for a year in Santa Cruz, Bolivia as a Rotary Club exchange student. He holds a B.A, M.A and M.S. in education from the University of Albany, Albany, New York. He taught English as a Foreign Language for a year in the Marie Curie Oberschule, Charlottenburg, West Berlin, and later English as a Second Language for many years in an upstate New York public school, grades kindergarten-12th grade. He is currently on the Board of Trustees of the Greene County Historical Society, located at the Bronck House and Museum, Coxsackie, New York.

Printed in the United States
by Baker & Taylor Publisher Services